to _____

from _____

Take Care Of ME from A to Z

by

Harriet Ziefert

dolls by

Tatiana Oles

🍎 Blue Apple Books

Text copyright © 2011 by Harriet Ziefert

Dolls copyright © 2011 by Tatiana Oles

Photographs by William Winburn

All rights reserved / CIP Data is available.

Published in the United States 2011 by

🍎 Blue Apple Books

515 Valley Street, Maplewood, NJ 07040

www.blueapplebooks.com

First Edition   03/11

Printed in China

ISBN: 978-1-60905-076-4

1 3 5 7 9 10 8 6 4 2

Everyone needs
a little T.L.C.

Follow these instructions
from A to Z.

A**dore me.**

Buzz me.

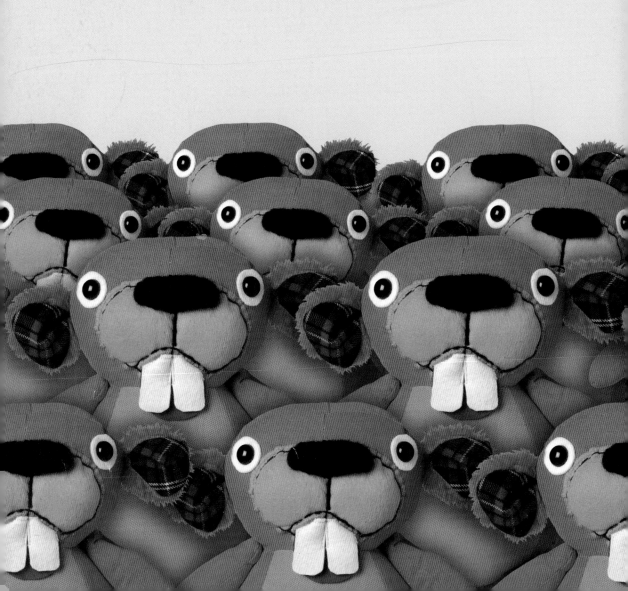

Choose me.

Dine
with me.

Eat
the crust
for me.

friend me.

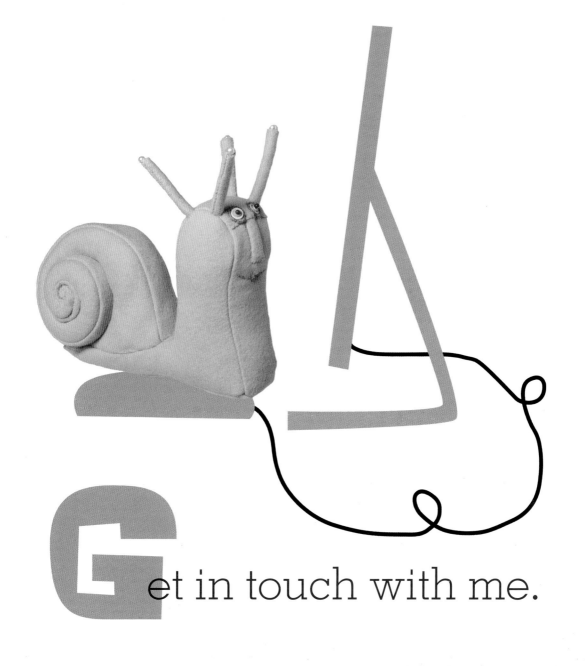

Get in touch with me.

*H*ug me.

Invite me.

Join me.

Kiss me.

Let me **L**ead.

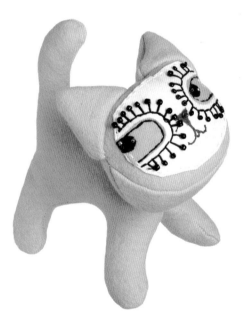

Make *M*usic with me.

otice me.

Outfit me.

Play
with me.

Quote me.

Read to me.

No 5

Sniff me.

Take care of me.

uncover me.

Vote
for me.

Warm me.

ecuse me!

Do Yoga with me.

Zip with me!